There's Greatness on the Inside

By Byron V. Garrett

There's greatness on the inside!

It all begins in the mind!

There's greatness on the inside.

It makes no difference
how big or small you are;

as long as you have a dream,
you will go far.

Dreams require hard work and patience to come true;

believe in yourself and your abilities too!

The real secret to success
is simply you being you!

There's greatness on the inside!

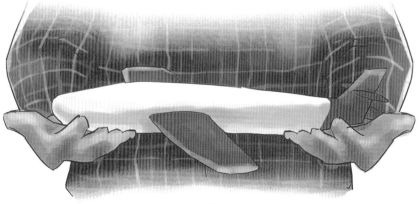

They don't lend a hand,
they don't help at all;
they want to see you
stumble and fall.

your family,

your teachers,

your neighbors,

and friends

they all believe you will succeed
and know that you can.

Life can be hard and challenging you see –

If you pay attention in school,
the smarter you will be!

You get to choose anything
that you want to be,

Just tell yourself
"it's up to me!".

The more you know, the more you will grow;
the more you learn, the more you will earn.

There's just no telling
how high you can go!

Today is a great day
to get on with your show!

There's greatness
on the inside.

Choose your future, beginning today
There is no reason for you to delay.

If the mind
can conceive it

and the heart
can believe it,

then the hands
can achieve it.

It all begins

in the mind.

There's greatness
on the inside.